Miss Adorabibble's Books

I love you a bushel and a peck

Written & Illustrated By

Miss Adorabibble

Published By

DeepRichDirt Publishing
DeepRichDirt.com

This is a work of fiction. Names, characters, places and incidents are the product of the author's imagination or are used fictitiously. Any resemblance to actual persons, events or locales is entirely coincidental. Although, it would be wonderful to have Farmer & Martha Primfill as neighbors!

Copyright © 2021 by
MissAdorabibble's books
; J. Stanfill ♡

All rights reserved. No part of this book may be reproduced or used in any manner without written permission of the copyright owner except for the use of quotations in a book review.

First edition March 2021
Design by Jobeth Stanfill

Dedicated to my very first grandbaby who stole my heart on October 4, 2020. 1 pound 9 ounces 12 & 3/4 inches long

Down a long and winding dirt road, past the dairy cows grazing on a hill and across from a newly painted yellow mailbox, was a very nice farm.

On this very nice farm there was a very smart garden filled with the most delicious vegetables. Beyond the smart garden was a lovely orchard with apple trees in four straight rows.

Beyond the four straight rows of apple trees grew a large and winding grape vine, heavy with clusters of purple grapes.

Farmer Primfill and his wife, Martha, loved their nice farm and took very good care of their dairy cows, smart garden, lovely orchard, big red barn and cozy farmhouse.

Farmer Primfill's wife, Martha Primfill, is a lovely woman with rosy cheeks, soft white hair and a very kind disposition. Martha loves to hang fresh clean laundry on the line, crochet warm sweaters, bake apple pies from scratch and make yummy homemade refrigerator pickles.

Every day, Farmer Primfill tends to his garden. He carefully pulls weeds, encourages bees to visit, and thoroughly waters the growing plants. Each type of vegetable is in its own straight row. At the beginning of each row there's a seed packet attached to a wooden stake.

Each seed packet has the name of the vegetable and a picture of **exactly** what the vegetable should look like. The vegetables feel a lot of pressure to be just like the vegetable on the seed packet.

After tending to the garden, Farmer Primfill tends to the orchard. It's very important to regularly fertilize and prune the apple trees. The orchard gets plenty of sun and has rich soil that drains well. Farmer Primfill removes the weeds around the trees and takes careful precautions to control unwanted pests.

Farmer Primfill starts up his old green tractor and attaches a brown wooden wagon. Inside the wagon sit four bushel baskets also known as peck baskets. One bushel equals four pecks. On this day, Farmer Primfill is going to harvest three bushel baskets of apples and one peck of big purple grape clusters.

The sun beams down on Farmer Primfill as he picks only the ripest of apples off the tree. He is very careful to properly pick each apple. A gentle roll upward and a twist is all it takes for the apple to come away from the spur of the branch. Farmer Primfill knows never to pull an apple straight off a branch and to never, ever shake a branch to make the apples fall off.

Before long, Farmer Primfill has three bushel baskets filled with apples and is ready to pick the ripe purple grape clusters. He always properly snips the grape cluster off the vine using sharp garden pruners. He gently places each juicy grape cluster in the bushel basket until it is about a peck full.

Farmer Primfill brings three bushel baskets of apples and one peck of grape clusters to the side of the white farmhouse. He sets them on the porch near the squeaky screen door. He is careful not to set the baskets too close to the squeaky screen door; otherwise Martha will have a troublesome time opening the door wide enough to pass through.

Martha is busy in the kitchen filling the large farmhouse sink with tepid water. She spreads a kitchen towel on top of the clean counter. Martha holds a corner of her favorite apron up and places a few apples in the fold, then carries them into the kitchen.

One by one, the apples plop into the water. Martha washes them thoroughly. The apples love to swim and bob in the warm water. After rinsing, she uses the kitchen towel to buff and polish each apple. When the last apple is polished, Martha places them in her favorite big, yellow mixing bowl.

The red apples are very proud of how eye-catching they look sitting in the large bowl.

Martha leans down and tells the apples, "I love you a bushel and a peck and a hug around the neck."

The apples feel special and very happy in their skin.

Martha drains the dirty water from the sink, then rinses, making sure all the dirt goes down the drain. She refills the sink with tepid water, then carries the peck of grape clusters into the kitchen.

Martha's kitchen is filled with busy hustle and bustle again . Many of the grape clusters chatter excitedly about things like jams, jellies, and delicious grape juice.

Martha is busy cleaning the grape clusters by swishing them around the water. She can't help but notice a grape with a sour look on her face. Curiously, Martha picks up the cluster and tenderly plucks the sour-faced grape off the cluster for a personal talk.

"Why the sour face?" asked Martha.

"I'm unhappy," sulked grape. "I do not feel like a grape and I don't want to be one either."

The other grapes on the cluster couldn't believe that the sour-faced grape had the **audacity** to complain about being a perfectly **fabulous** grape! The other grapes couldn't believe the sour grape had the **audacity** to not get excited about jams, jellies, and delicious grape juice!

According to the other grapes, the sour-faced grape **looked** like a perfectly **fabulous** grape. Secretly, on the inside, Grape felt pleasantly dry with charming wrinkles. The sour-faced grape was **not** happy in her skin. Grape knew she was **not** meant to hang on a cluster with other grapes. Grape knew she should be in the container with the other dry and wrinkly grapes called "raisins." Grape **identified** as a raisin.

Martha knew EXACTLY what to do.

"It's **ok** to feel different. It's **ok** not to feel excited talking about jams, jellies and grape juice" said Martha to Grape.

"I think I can help!" exclaimed Martha as she placed a sheet of parchment paper atop a baking sheet and set the oven to 200 degrees Fahrenheit.

She confidently set Grape on the baking sheet. Grape enjoyed the warmth of the oven as she dried out and noticed that she was getting the most charming wrinkles. Four hours passed and Martha took Grape out of the oven and let her cool off. Grape was **thrilled** that she looked on the **outside** exactly how she felt on the **inside**.

Grape decided to change her name to "Raisin" and **finally** felt very happy in her skin

Martha told Raisin, "I love you a bushel and a peck and a hug around the neck!"

Farmer Primfill decided to venture out to the garden to harvest some ripe vegetables. Not all vegetables ripen at the same time. Not all vegetables in the garden are even vegetables. Some vegetables are actually fruit, even though some people refer to them as vegetables. Farmer Primfill only harvests fruits and vegetables that are ripe and ready to be picked.

Today, ripe tomatoes and cucumbers will be picked. Farmer Primfill knows the correct way to pick all of the fruits and vegetables in the garden. To pick tomatoes, Farmer Primfill grasps the fruit firmly with one hand and holds the stem in his other, then gently pulls. After the tomato is picked off the vine, it is carefully placed in the bushel basket. Farmer Primfill fills one bushel basket full of tomatoes.

Cucumbers are next. Farmer Primfill uses garden pruners to cut the ripe cucumbers off the vine, leaving about an inch of the stem attached. Martha will remove the stem during the cleaning process. Farmer Primfill fills half a bushel or two pecks of cucumbers.

Farmer Primfill carries each bushel basket onto the large porch and places them near the screen door. Once again, he is careful not to set the bushel baskets too close to the screen door; otherwise Martha will have a troublesome time opening the door wide enough to pass through.

Today Martha will wash the tomatoes. The cucumbers will have to wait until tomorrow. Martha really enjoys washing the tomatoes. She loves watching the brilliant color bloom bright red as the dirt slides off. Martha fills the sink with lukewarm water and places the tomatoes gently in for a bath. Martha notices one of the tomatoes looks **very** grumpy. Martha very cautiously picks the tomato out of the water and dries him off.

"You look **very** unhappy and grumpy," said Martha to the tomato.

"I just **don't** feel comfortable in my skin," Tomato said with a huff.

Martha couldn't understand why the tomato felt the way that he did. Tomato was a stupendous red tomato. Martha knew Tomato would shine all sparkly clean after being buffed with a kitchen towel. Knowing these things did not change Tomato's grouchy mood.

Tomato did his best to explain that he **was** very happy with his gorgeous red color, and that he was going to **loveeeee** being buffed to a dazzling shine. Tomato just didn't feel like he **belonged** with the other tomatoes. He didn't feel like a tomato on the **inside.** He didn't think like the other tomatoes or get excited talking about things like zesty spaghetti sauce and bacon, lettuce and tomato sandwiches. It wasn't his dream to be filled with tuna salad.

The other tomatoes couldn't believe that he had the **audacity** to not think the way they did, and had the **audacity** to not get excited about things like zesty spaghetti sauce, delectable BLT sandwiches or being stuffed full with tantalizing tuna salad..

Tomato grumbled that he just wasn't happy in his skin.

Martha noticed how longingly Tomato looked at the big bowl of apples. He was round just like they were and he was red just like they were. He even had a stem just like they did. Tomato explained to Martha that even though he was a tomato he **identified** as an apple.

Martha knew EXACTLY what to do.
Martha explained to tomato that it was OK to feel different on the **inside** than you looked on the outside. Martha carried Tomato over to the big bowl of red apples and placed him on top.

The apples were very happy to meet Tomato and commented on how exquisite his red skin was. Tomato smiled and felt **very** happy in his skin.

"I love you a bushel and a peck and a hug around the neck," said Martha.

Tomato smiled.

It is almost the weekend and Martha is going to make one of Farmer Primfill's favorite snacks, homemade refrigerator pickles! He loves the tang of the garlic and apple cider vinegar on his tongue. Martha must shoo Farmer Primfill out of the kitchen and get started. She opens the screen door and brings in two pecks of cucumbers to be washed. The sink is filled once again with slightly warm water, and all the cucumbers tumble in as Martha tips the bushel basket and pours.

The cucumbers bob and float as Martha swishes and swooshes the water, making sure each cucumber is thoroughly wet. Martha bends over and grabs the soft vegetable brush that she keeps under the sink. She scrubs each cucumber clean, which makes them laugh and giggle, then lays them on a soft kitchen towel to air dry.

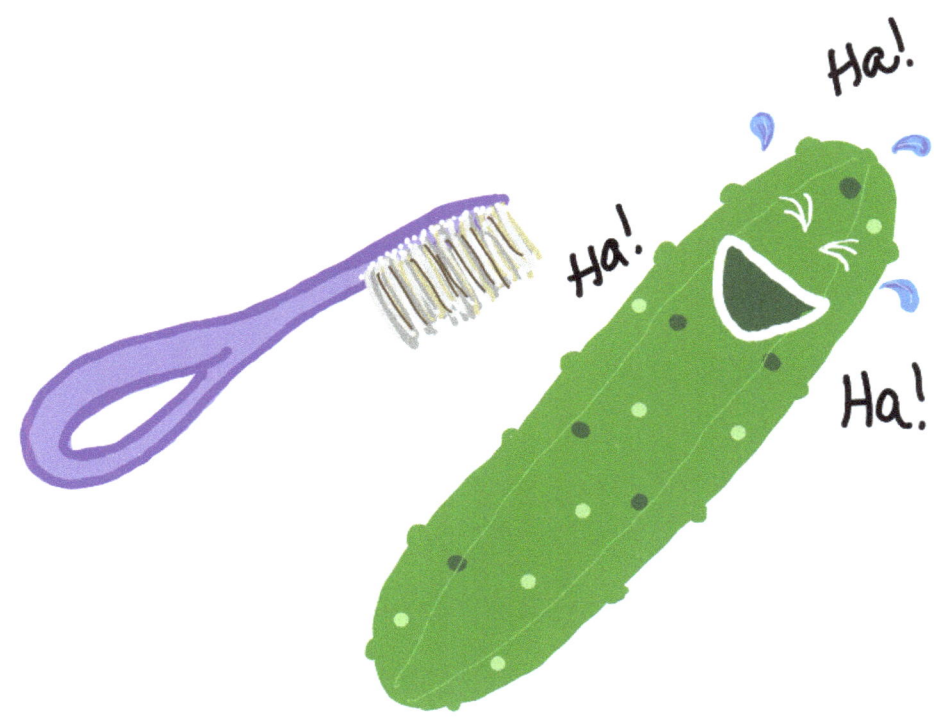

Martha always follows her recipe for homemade refrigerator pickles.

> Homemade Refrigerator Pickles
> 1 sweet Vidalia onion
> fresh dill weed
> apple cider vinegar
> garlic
> pickling salt
> whole black peppercorns
> whole mustard seeds
> red pepper flakes
> cold water

Martha walks over to the pantry and grabs a half gallon glass jar with a metal lid. She sets the jar and lid on the counter. In the jar, Martha packed onion slices, sprigs of dill, mustard seed and started inserting the excited cucumbers while the water, garlic, and other spices simmered in a sauce pan on the stove top.

One by one, Martha placed the cucumbers into the jar. The cucumbers were very enthusiastic anticipating their warm garlic and dill bath that would fill the jar. All the cucumbers that is, except for one. One frumpy faced, extra bumpy, misshaped, prickly cucumber with a peculiar looking stem. The frumpy, bumpy cucumber stood on the red and white kitchen towel and pouted.

"Well there little one, why so glum?" asked Martha.

The frumpy, bumpy cucumber looked up at Martha and burst into tears.

"The other cucumbers are laughing at me because I don't look like them and I do **not** want to change into a refrigerator pickle!" sobbed the frumpy, bumpy cucumber.

"If I have to change," explained Cucumber, "I will **not** feel comfortable in my skin."

The other cucumbers rolled their eyes and couldn't believe that the humdrum cucumber had the **audacity** to be content being a frumpy, bumpy, misshapen cucumber with an unsightly looking stem!

"Blah!" said a cucumber.
"Yuck!" said another.

The cucumbers in the jar snickered and whispered how homely he was.

Martha knew EXACTLY what to do!
She gently picked up the frumpy, bumpy cucumber off the kitchen towel and placed him in a cozy bowl to meet some new friends.

"Hello!" said Carrot.
"Hello!" said Potato.
"Hello!" said Celery.

Cucumber smiled at his new friends and said, "Hello!"

Cucumber looked different than his new friends and that was ok because they liked cucumber just the way he was. Cucumber felt accepted and appreciated.

Cucumber felt exceptionally happy in his skin.

Martha leaned over the bowl and said, "I love you a bushel and a peck and a hug around the neck."

Martha hurried back to the big jar filled with sweet Vidalia onion slices, fresh dill weed sprigs, and a few extremely embarrassed cucumbers. They felt very bad at how they treated the frumpy, bumpy cucumber.

Martha sighed and place her hands on her hips; she knew EXACTLY what to do. She removed the simmering sauce pan filled with water, apple cider vinegar, pickling salt, peppercorns, mustard seeds, and red pepper flakes, from the stove top. She carefully poured the scrumptious smelling warm liquid into the jar.

This felt absolutely **divine** to the cucumbers in the jar. The cucumbers felt very comfortable in their skin. Martha twisted the lid on the jar and placed it on the top shelf in the refrigerator.

The cucumbers snuggled in the jar for a nap. It will take about 24 hours to turn the cucumbers into refrigerator pickles.

As Martha closed the refrigerator door, she heard the sleepy cucumbers yawn and say, "We love you a bushel and a peck and a hug around the neck."

Martha smiled, and felt very happy in her skin.

CPSIA information can be obtained
at www.ICGtesting.com
Printed in the USA
LVHW050314140223
739459LV00008B/55